ISBN: 0-7172-8805-6

Disney's DuckTales

Christmas at the NORTH POLE

When Donald Duck decided to take a trip around the world, he arranged for his nephews Huey, Dewey, and Louie to stay with their Uncle Scrooge. The boys enjoyed their visit until the day before Christmas.

"Christmas won't be the same without Uncle
Donald," Dewey said sadly.

"We don't even know where he is,"
sighed Louie.

Just then Huey saw the postman outside.

Huey ran outside and came back
waving a letter. "It's from Uncle
Donald!" he shouted.
"Open it!" cried his brothers.

"*Dear Boys,*" Huey said, reading the letter.
"*I miss you. I am at the North Pole. Please ask
Uncle Scrooge to fly everyone here so we can
spend Christmas together. Love, Uncle Donald.*"
"But Christmas is tomorrow!" cried Louie.

"We have to find Uncle Scrooge,
and fast!" shouted Dewey. "Let's go!"
   The boys were sliding down the banister
when Webby, the housekeeper's niece, saw
them. "What's the hurry, guys?" she asked.

Huey showed
Webby the letter.

"Can I go, too?" she asked.

"Sure," answered Louie. "Uncle Donald
invited everyone."

"What are we waiting for? Let's ask Uncle
Scrooge!" said Webby.

Uncle Scrooge was in his study with Duckworth, the butler, when the kids burst in the room.

"Uncle Scrooge! Can we go to the North Pole for Christmas?" they shouted.

"The North Pole?" Scrooge said in disbelief.

Louie showed Scrooge the letter from Donald.

"Hmmm," said Scrooge as he read the letter. "Christmas is tomorrow. And plane fuel costs money, you know."

Then he saw a note at the bottom of the letter. It read: *P.S. Tell Uncle Scrooge he can look for gold at the North Pole.*

"Gold!" cried Scrooge. He sent for Mrs. Beakley, the housekeeper.

"Mrs. Beakley, I need
you to pack warm sweaters
and hats and socks,"
Scrooge told her. "And be
ready to leave in an hour."

"Whatever for?" she asked.

"We're spending Christmas at the North Pole,"
Scrooge explained.

"Yippee!" cheered the boys. Webby gave
Uncle Scrooge a kiss.

"This will be the best Christmas ever,"
Dewey said as they all ran upstairs.

In their room, the boys began to pack.

"Now, we have to take the important stuff. Like our skis," said Louie.

"And our toboggans," added Huey.

"Don't forget our skates," Dewey reminded them.

Meanwhile, Mrs. Beakley and Webby were busy, too. Mrs. Beakley packed her warmest dress.

"We must take the Christmas presents," she told Webby.

"And we have to take the tree," Webby replied.

Duckworth was busy packing, too. He neatly folded his warmest butler's uniform and put it into his suitcase.

When Duckworth was finished, he telephoned Scrooge's pilot, Launchpad McQuack.

"Duckworth speaking," the butler said. "Please have Mr. Scrooge McDuck's plane ready for a flight to the North Pole right away."

"The North Pole?" Launchpad asked. "All right. But I wish we were going to the beach instead."

Launchpad got the plane ready.

"I wish McDuck would get a new plane," he said to himself. "Whenever something goes wrong, McDuck always thinks it's *my* fault."

Soon Scrooge and the family were ready. As they boarded the plane, Launchpad loaded all their bags.

"Do you really need all these things?" he asked.

"Of course," said Louie. "We *have* to bring our skis and toboggans and skates to the North Pole."

"And we *have* to bring our Christmas presents. And presents belong under a tree," added Webby.

"Silly me," said Launchpad. "For a moment I thought you were bringing too much!"

When Launchpad finished, he boarded the plane and started the engine. Soon the ducks were flying high, winging their way to the North Pole.

"Whew!" Launchpad said to himself. "I was afraid we wouldn't get off the ground because we have so much stuff. It should be smooth sailing from here."

But Launchpad spoke too soon. Suddenly
the plane began to shake and sway. Boxes started
bouncing around inside.

"Stop fooling around up there!" Scrooge
shouted to his pilot.

"It's not me!" cried Launchpad. "It's the plane."

Launchpad tried to control the plane. But it twisted and looped right into a snowstorm!

"Wheee!" shouted Webby and the boys. "This is fun!"

Launchpad almost had the plane
straightened out when he had to swerve
to avoid a flock of birds.

With that, even the kids began to feel dizzy. But suddenly Launchpad was able to pull the plane out of the spin and get it back on course.

"Pretty exciting," said Launchpad. "But I was in control the whole time."

As they flew north, the landscape below them began to change. It was winter everywhere!

"It won't be long now," Launchpad called out. "Next stop, the North Pole!"

Again, the pilot spoke too soon. He was so busy looking at the scenery…

…that he didn't notice the mountain of ice in front of him. *Crack!*

"Hold on, everyone!" Launchpad shouted.

He tried to pull the plane up, but soon realized that one of the wings had been damaged.

"Fasten your seat belts. I'll have to make an emergency landing," Launchpad called to his passengers.

The ducks gripped their seats as they landed. Launchpad was able to set the plane down on a large sheet of ice.

The pilot helped everyone out of the plane.
They were all happy to be on the ground.

"It might take me all night to repair the
damage," said Launchpad.

"You blockhead!" cried
Scrooge. "It's Christmas
Eve! We're going to miss
spending Christmas
with Donald."

Mrs. Beakley suggested that they put up a tent,
unload the presents, and decorate the tree.

"If we have to spend Christmas here, we might
as well enjoy it," she said.

After dinner, while Launchpad worked on the plane, everyone gathered around a campfire. They told stories, sang carols, and looked so happy that some animals came by to join in the fun.

"This is turning out to be a wonderful Christmas," Scrooge said. "I only wish that we could be with Donald."

"We can!" called Launchpad. "The plane's fixed." He went to help his passengers gather their things when he heard another loud crack!

The ice was breaking up—and the plane was drifting away! Launchpad quickly leaped over the crack to get to the plane.

"Try to jump!"
shouted Launchpad.

"We'll never make it," answered Scrooge. "The crack is too wide." Luckily, Huey had an idea. He gathered the animals together and explained his plan to them.

The animals understood. One by one
they jumped into the water. They were
making a bridge!

The travelers gathered all their things.
Then they carefully crossed the icy water
over the backs of the animals.

"Thank you!" they called to the
animals. "Merry Christmas!"

It wasn't easy, but soon the plane was in the air again. The sun was rising, and it was Christmas morning.

Huey, Dewey, and Louie were sad. "We're very late–what if we miss Uncle Donald?" worried Huey.

"Cheer up, fellas," said Launchpad. "I've got some good news."

"I've just heard from Donald on the radio.
We will be meeting him in five minutes!"

"Oh, boy!" cried Huey.

"We'd better decorate the tree again," said
Louie, "so it's ready for Uncle Donald."

Soon they could see Donald waving to them from below.

The boys waved back. They were all tired, but happy. "Now that we're all together," Dewey said, "it really feels like Christmas at last."